Yosemite's Songster

One Coyote's Story

Ginger Wadsworth

ILLUSTRATED BY Daniel San Souci

YOSEMITE CONSERVANCY

Yosemite National Park

In memory of our friend Steven Medley, the long-time director and publisher of the Yosemite Association. This book about coyotes in his beloved Yosemite National Park was Steve's idea that we are honored to fulfill. —G.W. and D.S.S.

The publisher wishes to thank the family of Donald Prevett for the generous donation that helped make this book possible.

YOSEMITE CONSERVANCY.

yosemiteconservancy.org

Yosemite Conservancy's Mission
Providing for Yosemite's future is our passion. We inspire people to support projects and programs that preserve and protect Yosemite National Park's resources and enrich the visitor experience.

Library of Congress Control Number 2012952115

Cover art: Daniel San Souci
Cover design: Nancy Austin
Interior design: Nancy Austin

ISBN 978-1-930238-34-3

Printed in Malaysia by TWP Sdn Bhd, February 2013

1 2 3 4 5 6 – 17 16 15 14 13

ON A SUNNY SPRING MORNING in Yosemite National Park,
Coyote and her mate stalk a squirrel on a hillside.

Suddenly a tower of granite topples above them,
starting a rock slide.

Within seconds,
rocks roll,
big and small,
smacking one another like spilled marbles.

CRASH! BLAM! SLAM!

Boulders bounce into a nearby stream
jammed with uprooted trees and plants.

Coyote leaps to the left;
her mate lunges to the right,
dodging the rumbling river of stones.

Dust flies from her furry coat
as Coyote runs and runs!

Coyote darts past Curry Village's canvas cabins.
She crosses a paved road.
A footpath brings Coyote to a brown-shingled home
shaded by two oaks.

She scoots beneath the house,
straight into one of her dens.

Coyote scratches and stirs up her dirt bed,
then circles around and around and around
before finally lying down.

With her tail wrapped across her nose,
Coyote sleeps alone.

Coyote wakes when it is dark.
She whines.

Hungry now, she trots up the road.
Shops, restaurants, the Indian Village, and the
    Visitor Center are closed.

A great horned owl hoots from a Jeffrey Pine.
After a late-night bicyclist pedals by,
Coyote sniffs around
but trashcans are sealed shut.

Just before sunrise,
Coyote points her muzzle sky-high.
She yips, yodels, and yowls.

Her mate does not answer.

Coyote dozes beneath an elderberry bush,
a perfect umbrella shading her
from the midday sun.

People are everywhere,
talking,
walking,
riding bicycles,
or peering out bus windows.
Backpackers hurry by,
eager to hike a distant trail.

A few fishermen work the Merced River all day.
Rubber boats float by,
filled with lively families wearing sunscreen
    and life jackets.

Coyote's pointed ears listen while she waits.

"Raise your hand if this is your first visit
to Yosemite National Park!"
A dozen hands go up.
A park ranger leads a nature walk
across a wooden sidewalk
built to protect this fragile, wet mountain meadow.

He pauses and points to Half Dome.
He turns to identify El Capitan.
Steller's jays swoop through the trees.

Everyone is looking up,
oohing, aahing
over waterfalls and granite cliffs,
and taking pictures.

No one spots the wild dog in the tall grasses.
Coyote crouches and creeps forward ... slowly.

Grasses part.
Two tiny ears appear.
Coyote pounces.
A field mouse makes a tasty snack.

After an afternoon of mousing,
Coyote slinks into the shade above the steepled
    Yosemite Valley Chapel.
She rests to the sounds of mule deer nipping
    grass nearby.

Below Coyote,
cars stop; doors slam.
Visitors hurry here and there
to photograph Yosemite Falls
in its spring glory.

The church organ starts up inside the chapel.
A newlywed couple and their guests file outside
to Coyote's lonely song
and the thunder of Yosemite Falls across the Valley.

"Look, Mom! Look over there! I see a coyote!"
A boy calls out from the open-air tram.
"Where?"
"Did he see a bear?"
"No!"
"Stop! Someone sees a bear."

The tram stops.
Excited visitors rush to one side,
speaking in languages from around the world.
"Oh, dear. I don't see it."
"Not a deer, my dear … a coyote."

The tram starts moving again, and the boy points.
"There! Over there!"
"Where?"
The tram rolls past Coyote
and the boy watches.

Families return to campgrounds, cafeterias,
    and hotels for dinner.
Coyote is still hungry.

She prowls the river's shore near the
    housekeeping cabins,
spying on her world with intense yellow eyes.
Perhaps she'll find a duck drifting downstream
or surprise a frog leaping from rock to rock.

She waits, watches, and listens
while her nose twitches, pulling in the night smells.

Twilight descends like a slowly lowering
    window shade,
casting shadows on rock walls
until Yosemite Valley is dark.

Coyote moves on to hunt alone.

Coyote circles a campground.
Excited children chatter as they help their parents
     unpack cars and put up tents.
Flashlights flicker like fireflies.
Hamburgers sizzle on smoky grills.

Days before,
a black bear lumbered by,
leaving her scent on the forest floor.

Coyote sniffs the air again and stops,
letting two skunks have the right of way.

Once again,
Coyote points her muzzle high.
Ai-yi-yi she yaps over and over.
Her music rides the winds,
still unanswered.

THAT NIGHT, Coyote follows the Merced River
to Sentinel Bridge.
On the east side of the stone bridge,
visitors gaze at Half Dome
and at the moon rising beyond the magnificent
    monolith.
Some click cameras.
Others hold hands.

On the west side, Coyote raises her muzzle high
and howls at the star-filled sky.

At last, a familiar yip returns her song!

Coyote sprints!
She passess house-sized boulders,
lopes past dogwood trees
and the sweeping drive of the Ahwahnee.

Beyond the glittery hotel,
Coyote finds her mate!
They touch noses
and whine greetings to one another.
Bushy tails wave up and down and back
    and forth.

Together at last,
the two coyotes tussle puppy-style
on the pine needle floor.

Coyote and her mate slip past Mirror Lake,
now pooled with spring snowmelt.
The seasonal lake reflects the surrounding cliffs
in the moonlight.

They zigzag higher.

From distant backpackers' camps,
dots of lights seem to wink at them
among the trees.

Rock climbers, roped tight to ledges halfway up
    Half Dome,
try to doze.

Far below them all, Yosemite Valley's lights fade.

The coyotes pause.
Ai-yi-yi.
Yip! Yip! Yee! they sing.

Other coyotes answer.
Sisters,
sons,
strangers,
and pack-mate pals sing echoing songs
of coyote life.

Ai-yi-yi.
Yip! Yip! Yee!

The Yosemite wilderness is never silent,
even after sunset.
Winds cruise through the trees,
stirring pinecones and sleepy birds.
Swaying rock towers groan.
Boulders shift,
slipping and sliding in their nighttime beds.
Mice squeak,
and mighty tree limbs creak.
Streams splash and waterfalls fall night and day.

On this moonlit night,
Coyote leads the way.
Slip, slap. Slip, slap. Slip, slap.
Eight coyote paws are on the move,
heading home to the Yosemite Valley.

AUTHOR'S NOTE

Just when you least expect it, you might hear a coyote yip and yap in the night or you might glimpse a wild-looking, bushy-tailed dog in your neighborhood, in an open space, in a crowded city, or even in a national park. Coyotes live in rural, suburban, and urban areas across America, and they are flourishing in Yosemite National Park as well.

The scientific name for coyotes is *Canis latrans,* which means "barking dog." Many live in pairs; some travel in small packs. Their territory, or the distance they travel within Yosemite and around the Sierra Nevada, depends on the available food, the time of year, and even the weather conditions in California's rugged mountains.

Arriving park visitors get a "Keep Wildlife Wild" bookmark with a coyote on the front. They are asked to stay a respectful distance from all the wildlife and to drive slowly in the park. They need to leash their pets all the time. No one should touch or feed any wild animal, big or small. Yosemite's coyotes primarily eat small rodents like ground squirrels and field mice. But they also scavenge for food, even if it is not healthy for them. Some have learned to beg for handouts at picnic sites, campgrounds, and alongside the roads. Eating "human" food causes coyotes to have digestive problems.

Watch for signs that alert visitors to coyote activity, such as a nearby den with pups. The mother and her mate might become aggressive if anyone gets too close. Instead, use your eyes, camera, and binoculars to discover a coyote mousing in a meadow, foraging for bird eggs, grasshoppers, caterpillars, frogs, and lizards, or gorging on ripe berries. The park's goal is to keep Yosemite safe for its human visitors as well as the many wild animals, including coyotes, that live there.

ACKNOWLEDGMENTS

Special thanks go to Tori Seher, wildlife biologist; Mary Kline, branch chief, Interpretive Services at Yosemite National Park; Camilla Fox, founding director of Project Coyote at www.projectcoyote.org; and my editor, Nicole Geiger. I appreciate everyone's help!
—Ginger Wadsworth